# The Gryphon Press

*—a voice for the voiceless—*

These books are dedicated to those who foster compassion toward all animals.

For Jeff Prine, a simply marvelous friend and connoisseur of canines. — *N.F.*

Thank you to my friend Risa Schwartz and her students at Mar Vista School
whose help was invaluable in the making of these illustrations. — *J.H.*

Printed in Canada by Friesens Corporation
Text set in Cochin by BookMobile Design and Publishing Services

Library of Congress Control Number: 2010928919
ISBN: 978-0-940719-11-8
3 5 7 9 10 8 6 4 2
A portion of profits from this book will be
donated to shelters and animal rescue societies.

*I am the voice of the voiceless:*
*Through me, the dumb shall speak;*
*Till the deaf world's ear be made to hear*
*The cry of the wordless weak.*

*— from a poem by Ella Wheeler Wilcox, early 20th-century poet*

*a gentle dog's rescue*

# Maggie's Second Chance

**written by Nancy Furstinger * illustrated by Joe Hyatt**

Maggie waited, watching the door. Her growing belly grumbled.
Where was her dinner?

Suddenly the door swung open. Maggie's tail spun
as she greeted her family. She nudged her empty bowl.

They didn't look at her. The woman picked up a box and left again.

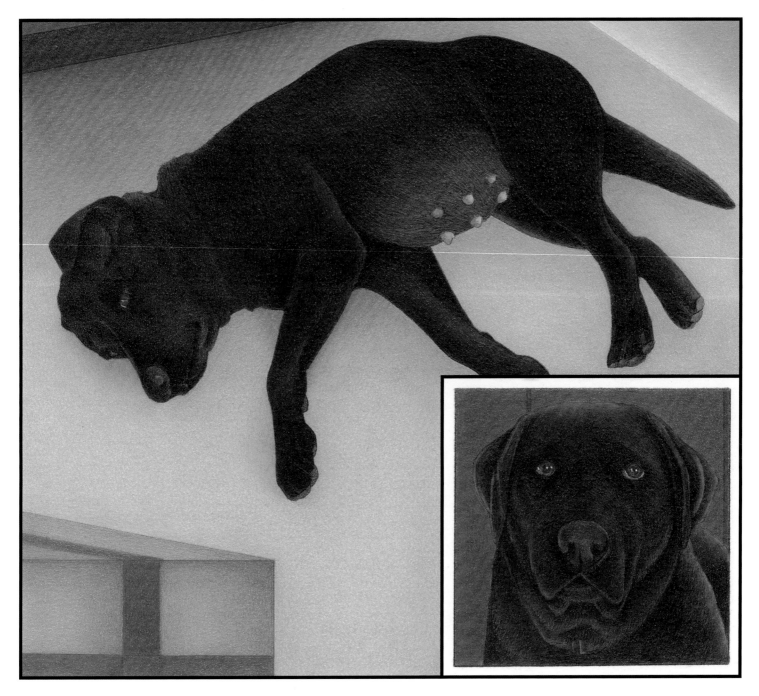

Maggie rolled over for a treat, but the boy grabbed a suitcase
instead of the dog biscuits. When the door slammed shut,
Maggie was alone.

She was alone as stars twinkled and then dimmed.
Logs in the woodstove turned to smoke.
Wind trailed icy fingers against the windows.

Maggie's big belly ached. She tried scratching at the door.
She slurped freezing toilet water.
Then she huddled in the bare room.

Maggie heard a key in the door. Had her family returned?
No. It was a stranger. When he looked at her,
he barked angry words into his phone.

Later, a man coaxed Maggie into the back of his van with treats.
"She's gonna deliver puppies any minute," he said to himself.

Maggie entered the place where dogs barked behind bars,
and she was taken to a large cage.

That night, Maggie's puppies were born. She nuzzled nine,
but pushed aside two. Their tiny hearts never made a single beat.

Busy hands reached into Maggie's cage.
They changed newspapers, weighed puppies, and filled bowls.

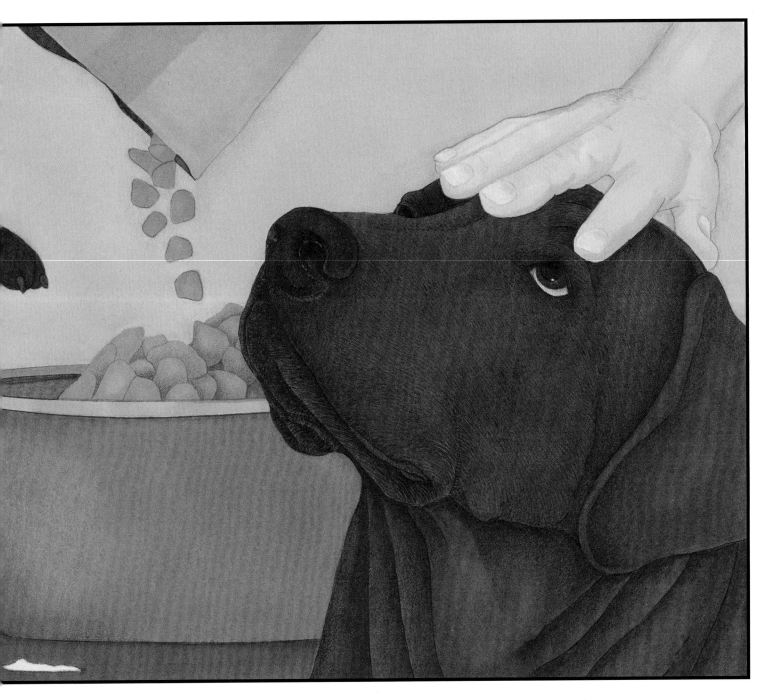

One pair of hands found time to pet Maggie.

A photographer snapped photos of Maggie and her puppies.
The photos appeared in the next day's newspaper. People saw them
and adopted Maggie's puppies, one by one.

No one glanced at Maggie. She was just another big black dog,
blending into the shadows.
A bit of the wag disappeared from her tail.

As a boy named Jeff recycled newspapers, he saw the photo of Maggie.
He tore out the photo and brought it to class.
"What happens if Maggie doesn't find a home?" Jeff asked his teacher.
When she told him, he asked, "Why does this dog have to die
just because she doesn't have a home by a certain time?"

Jeff said, "If she could have a place to stay long enough,
I bet someone would adopt her. Can't we do something?"
His classmates agreed. They said,
"Maggie deserves a second chance!"

They brainstormed a plan, a big plan for an animal shelter.
Their teacher arranged for the plan to be discussed
at the next town council meeting.

She asked permission for the class to attend the meeting.
The students and some of their parents came to the meeting and talked
about why their town needed an animal shelter. The plan passed!

News of the decision to build an animal shelter made the front page
of the town newspaper. Readers donated land, supplies, and money.
Volunteers helped build the shelter.
They gave with their hearts and hands.

The kids named their shelter Pooch Pals.
When the sign went up on the finished sanctuary, everyone —
Jeff, his teacher, and the whole class —
was ready to take a bus to begin the rescue work.

At the pound, a red X had been marked on Maggie's chart.
"I'm sorry, girl," the woman with the kind hands said as she petted
Maggie. "There simply aren't enough homes for good dogs."
She snapped a collar and leash on Maggie. She swiped at her eyes
as she led the dog down the hallway.

Jeff raced inside, ahead of the others.
"We've come for the dogs no one wants.
We have a shelter for them! Where's Maggie?"
The receptionist quickly took the microphone and called into it,
"Bring Maggie right now. There's a home for her."

Maggie whined when she heard her name called.
She tugged free of her leash and scampered around the corner
toward someone who was shouting "Maggie!"
—and she ran into Jeff's welcoming hug.

# Adopting a Dog

If you are searching for a dog to be your newest family member, please look for that special dog at your local animal shelter or rescue group. There you will find a furry friend like Maggie, who is waiting to join you on a lifelong adventure.

When you adopt a dog, you'll be saving two lives: the life of your new pet and the life of another homeless dog who will fill the empty spot in the shelter. Your dog likely will have been neutered or spayed at the shelter, but if not, help stamp out pet overpopulation by having your female spayed or your male neutered. This simple, safe surgery will prevent your dog from becoming a parent and adding more dogs who need homes to your community.

# This Book Is Based On a True Story

**Dalhart Animal Wellness Group and Sanctuary** was begun in 2003 by four fourth-grade students who were upset about dogs being euthanized in their town. They went to their teacher, Diane Trull, who explained that with seven puppies and kittens born for every one human, there were not enough homes to go around. Their tiny Texas pound was killing seven hundred dogs each year. The students refused to accept this tragedy. Determined, the students and their teacher went to the city council and convinced the members to set up a no-kill shelter. Diane Trull, her husband, Mark, and their family worked with children age nine to eighteen to run the sanctuary, as they do today. With very limited resources, the children began to pick up dogs and cats from the pound, have them checked by local vets, vaccinated, and most important, spayed or neutered. DAWGS (Dalhart Animal Wellness Group and Sanctuary) has found homes for more than five thousand needy animals. The DAWGS kids believe that "all dogs are equal and each one has a special gift to give."

The author will donate a percentage of her royalties to DAWGS.

# Maggie Is a Real Dog Rescued by the Author

After Maggie gave birth to fifteen puppies (the fifteenth did not survive), her owners advertised her as "free to a good home." Neighbors brought her home, but a few months later they moved, leaving Maggie behind in an empty house. The author rescued this Labrador-shepherd mix, intending to foster her until a forever home was found. Fortunately, she flunked Fostering 101: Maggie was the dog she never knew she was searching for. Renamed Jolly for her cheerful disposition, she joined the author's two rescued dogs and a warren of house rabbits.

# Resources

To search for a dog to adopt in your own neighborhood, go to **www.petfinder.com**.

You can find more information about pet adoption at these sites:

* www.dawgsntexas.com

* adoptions.bestfriends.org

* www.aspca.org/adoption

* www.humanesociety.org/issues/adopt